THE ADVENTURES OF SNOWMAN

MW00902272

BY RICHARD S. HARTMETZ

Published in 2019, by Starry Night Publishing.Com
Rochester, New York

THE STORY OF FROSTY THE SNOWMAN

First brought to life as a Christmas song written by Walter "Jack" Rollins and Steve Nelson in 1949, the song was first recorded by cowboy legend Gene Autry in 1950, following quickly on his success with *Rudolph, the Red-Nosed Reindeer* the previous year. Later that same year, the song was recorded by actor Jimmy Durante, then Nat "King" Cole and Guy Lombardo.

In 1951, the story of Frosty had become so popular, that Frosty became a Little Golden Book, followed soon after by an adaptation by Dell Comics. Dell continued the tradition of their Frosty comics for a decade, bringing them to an end in 1961. The fabulous Dell Comics are the source for the fifty stories in this collection.

In 1969, CBS aired the now-famous Rankin-Bass animated special, *Frosty the Snowman,* followed by *Frosty's Winter Wonderland* in 1976 and Rudolph and *Frosty's Christmas in July* in 1979. Jackie Vernon played the voice of Frosty in all three of these specials.

Now, presented here, for the first time ever, in 370 pages, are the fifty greatest adventures of one of everyone's favorite Christmas characters, Frosty the Snowman!

FROSTY THE SNOWMAN

8

10

16

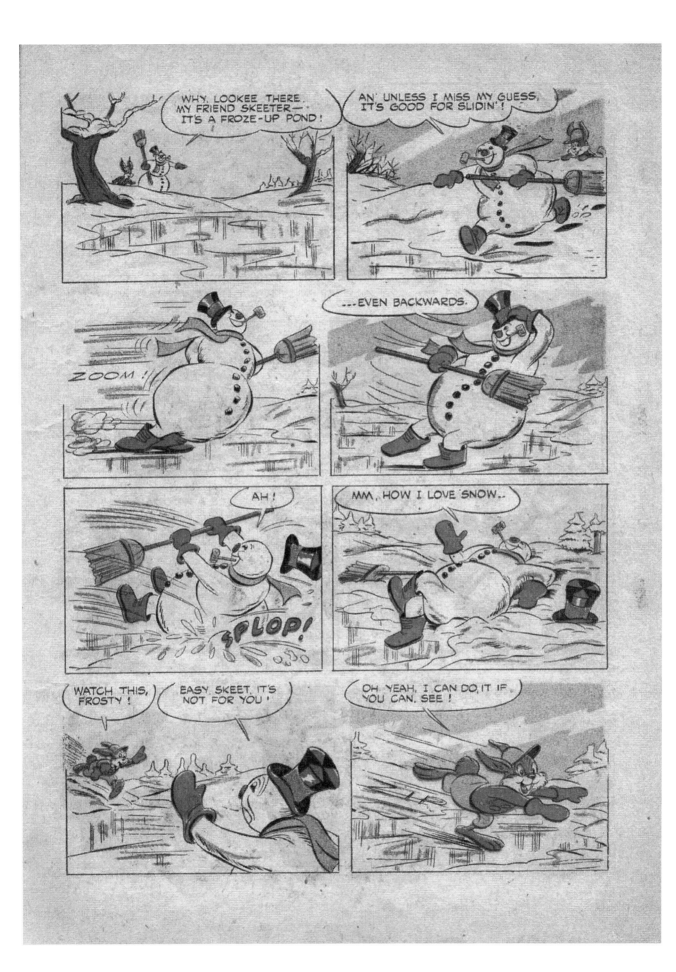

17

21

23

25

26

28

29

30

31

33

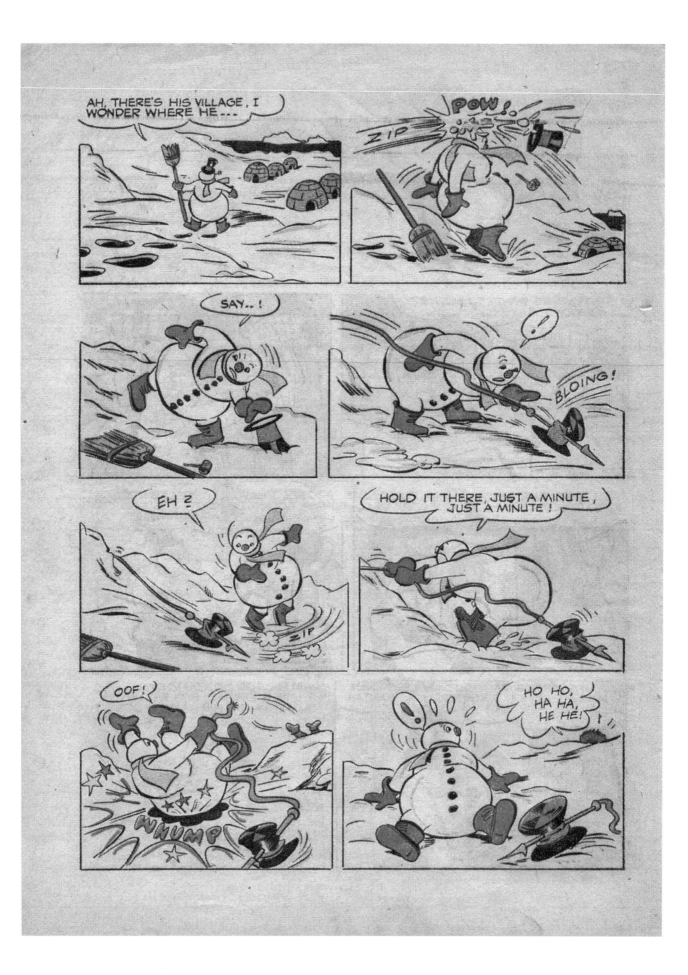

36

41

42

43

44

45

47

48

49

51

55

56

57

60

61

63

65

76

81

90

93

94

97

99

101

DELL COMICS ARE GOOD COMICS

105

106

111

115

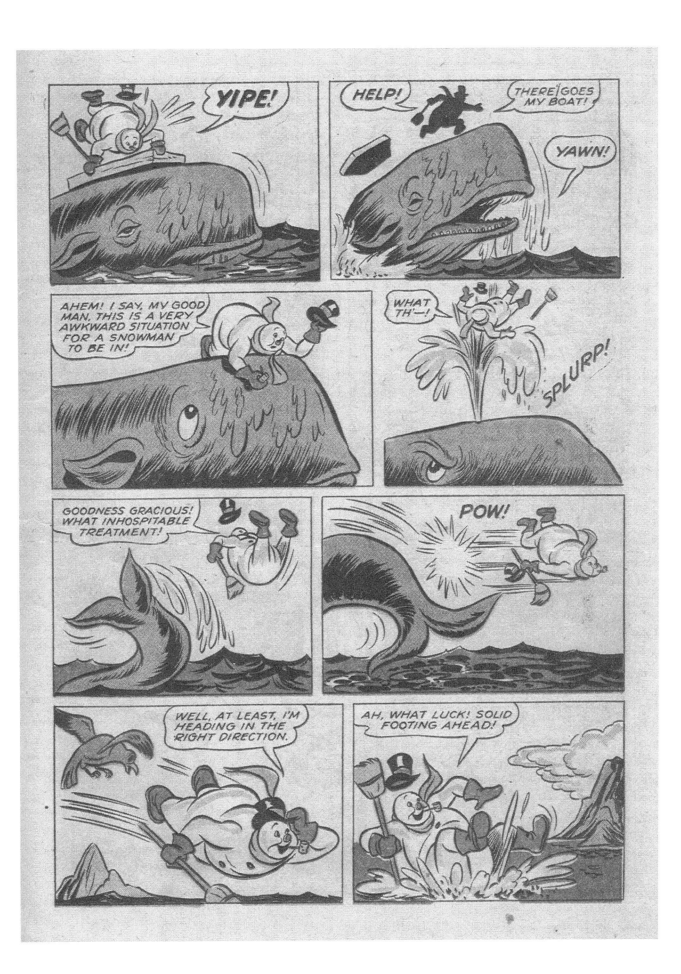

121

122

123

126

128

130

135

140

145

163

174

175

178

179

183

185

188

I WAS SO TIRED WHEN I FINISHED THAT I DECIDED TO TAKE FORTY WINKS THERE IN THE SHOP.

SO I CRAWLED UNDER THE BLANKET AND IMMEDIATELY WENT OFF TO SLEEP.

IT WASN'T LONG BEFORE SANTA CAME IN WITH SEVERAL HELPERS...

AND INTO HIS BAG I WENT ALONG WITH ALL THE OTHER TOYS!

THE REINDEER WERE HITCHED TO THE SLEIGH, THE WHIP CRACKED, AND OFF WE WENT!

WELL, IT WASN'T LONG BEFORE I WAS PLACED, STILL ASLEEP, UNDER A CHRISTMAS TREE!

YOU CAN IMAGINE MY SURPRISE WHEN I WAS AWAKENED!

I DIDN'T KNOW WHAT TO DO....SO TO PLAY SAFE, I DID NOTHING, NOT EVEN 'MA-MA'!

199

208

211

212

214

216

219

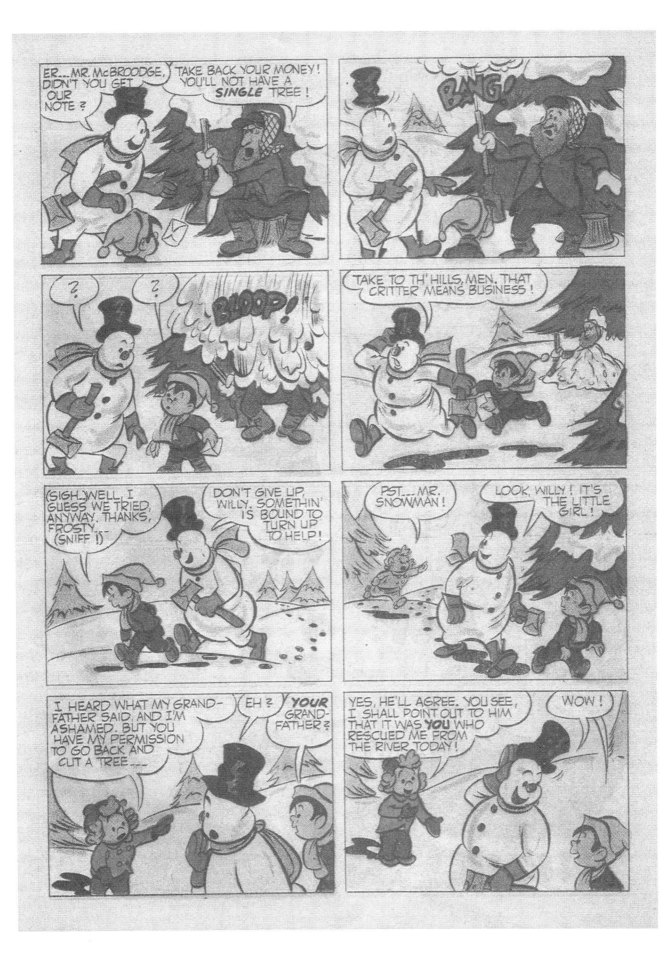

221

222

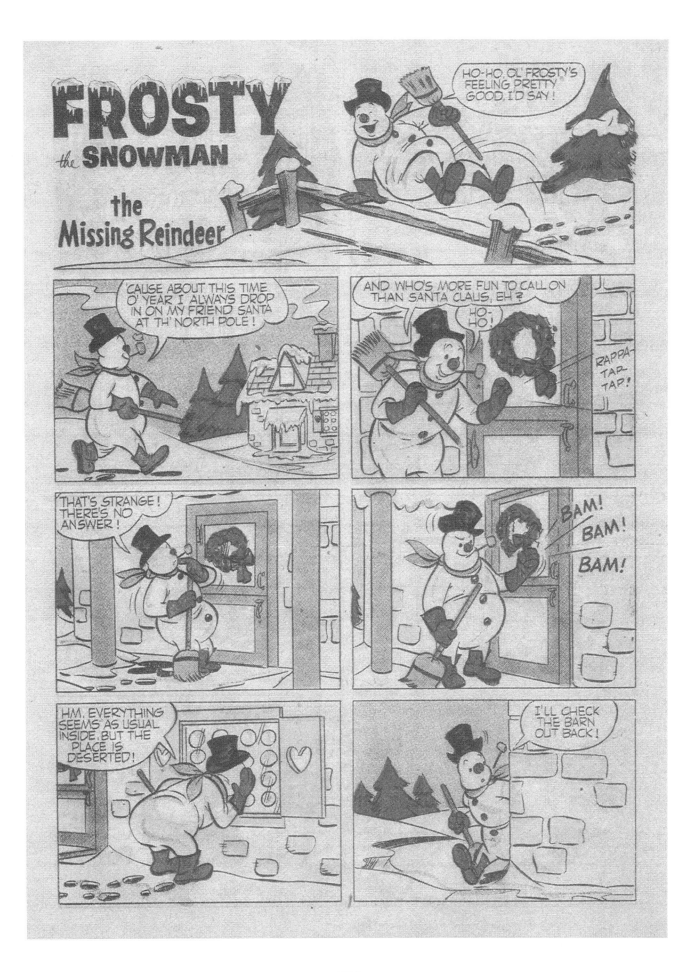

226

227

232

240

244

245

246

247

250

251

258

260

262

263

264

265

267

FROSTY the SNOWMAN

Christmas Spirit

FROSTY THE SNOWMAN, No. 1065, Dec.-Feb., 1960. Published by Dell Publishing Co., Inc., 750 Third Avenue, New York 17, N. Y. George T. Delacorte, Jr., Publisher; Helen Meyer, President; Paul R. Lilly, Executive Vice-President; Harold Clark, Vice-Pres.-Advertising Director; Albert P. Delacorte, Treasurer. All rights reserved throughout the world. Authorized edition. Designed and produced by Western Printing & Litho-graphing Co. Printed in U.S.A. Copyright © 1959, by Hill & Range Songs, Inc.

269

271

272

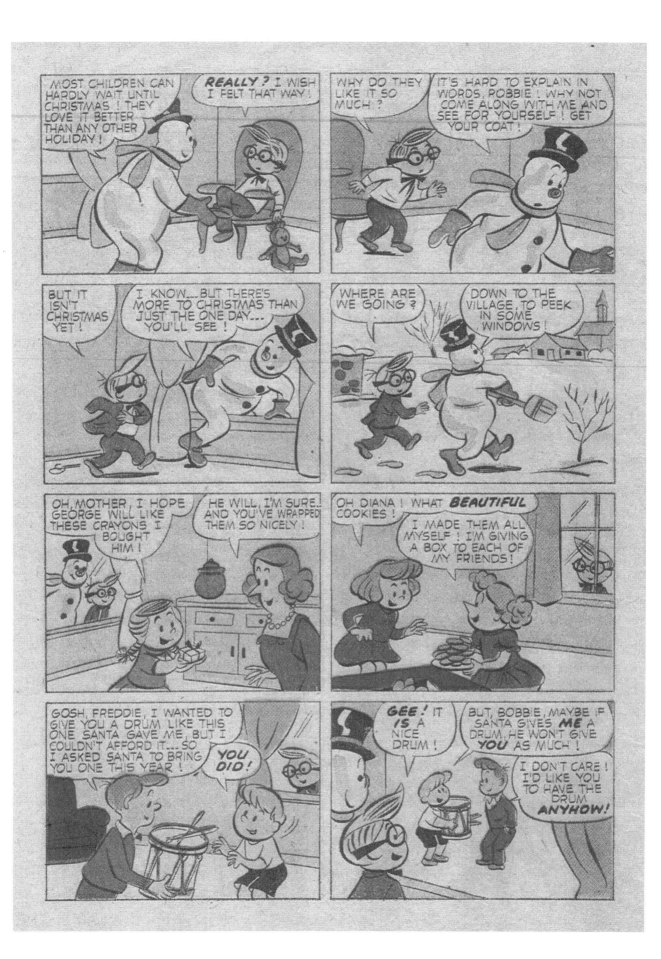

274

276

FROSTY the SNOWMAN

The Bewitched Forest

279

282

285

288

290

294

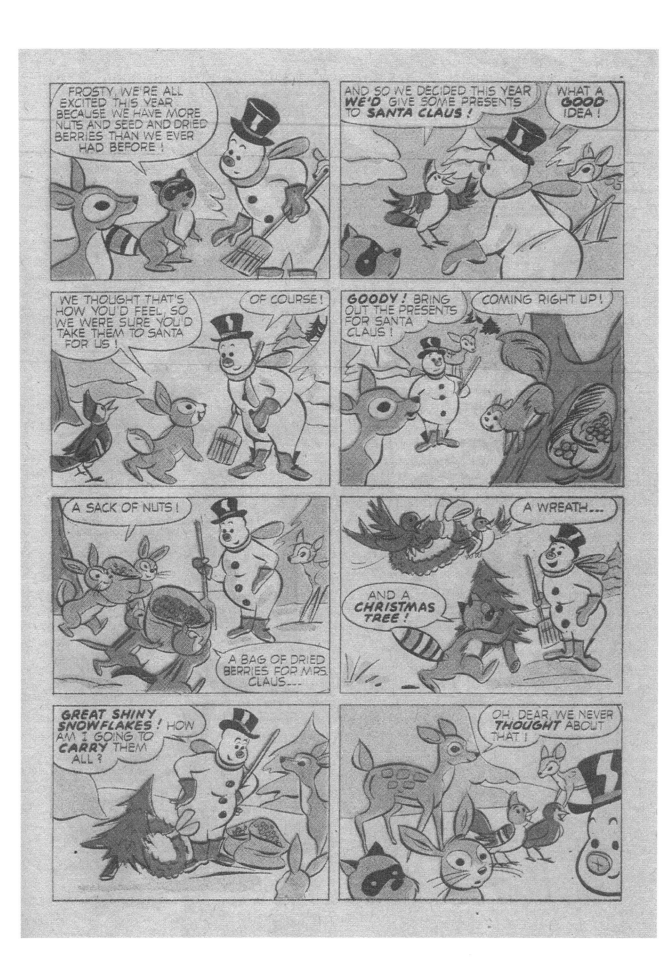

298

FROSTY THE SNOWMAN, No. 1153, Dec.-Feb., 1961. Published by Dell Publishing Co., Inc., 750 Third Avenue, New York 17, N. Y. George T. Delacorte, Jr., Publisher; Helen Meyer, President; Executive Vice-Presidents, William F. Callahan, Jr., Paul R. Lilly; Harold Clark, Vice-President-Advertising Director; Bryce L. Holland, Vice-President; Albert P. Delacorte, Treasurer. All rights reserved throughout the world. Authorized edition. Designed and produced by Western Printing & Lithographing Co. Printed in U.S.A. Copyright © 1960, by Hill & Range Songs, Inc.

305

309

314

316

318

319

FROSTY the SNOWMAN

The Lonely Donkey

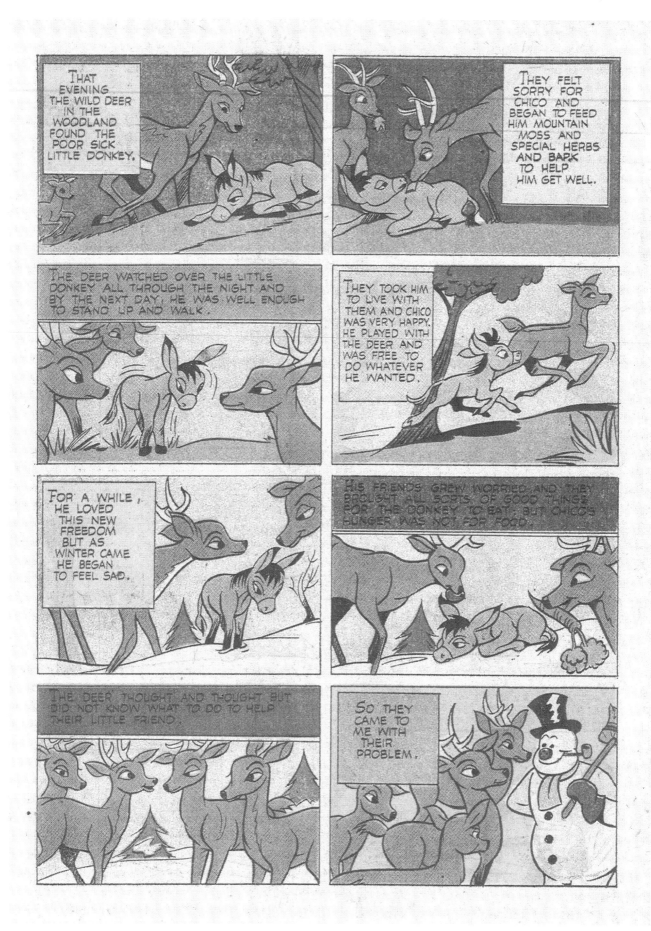

THAT EVENING THE WILD DEER IN THE WOODLAND FOUND THE POOR SICK LITTLE DONKEY.

THEY FELT SORRY FOR CHICO AND BEGAN TO FEED HIM MOUNTAIN MOSS AND SPECIAL HERBS AND BARK TO HELP HIM GET WELL.

THE DEER WATCHED OVER THE LITTLE DONKEY ALL THROUGH THE NIGHT AND BY THE NEXT DAY, HE WAS WELL ENOUGH TO STAND UP AND WALK.

THEY TOOK HIM TO LIVE WITH THEM AND CHICO WAS VERY HAPPY, HE PLAYED WITH THE DEER AND WAS FREE TO DO WHATEVER HE WANTED.

FOR A WHILE, HE LOVED THIS NEW FREEDOM BUT AS WINTER CAME HE BEGAN TO FEEL SAD.

HIS FRIENDS GREW WORRIED AND THEY BROUGHT ALL SORTS OF GOOD THINGS FOR THE DONKEY TO EAT, BUT CHICO'S HUNGER WAS NOT FOR FOOD.

THE DEER THOUGHT AND THOUGHT BUT DID NOT KNOW WHAT TO DO TO HELP THEIR LITTLE FRIEND.

SO THEY CAME TO ME WITH THEIR PROBLEM.

324

329

335

336

337

338

340

342

343

345

346

348

351

352

354

355

356

"IT'S ALL VERY SIMPLE. OUR KING MARRIED A BEAUTIFUL PRINCESS FROM A LAND FAR SOUTH WHERE THERE IS NO SNOW."

"QUEEN DIANE IS LOVELY IN EVERY WAY, BUT FOR SOME STRANGE REASON, SHE *HATES* SNOW."

"THE VERY FIRST TIME A SNOWFLAKE FELL ON HER, SHE HAD A TANTRUM! AND IF THE LEAST LITTLE SNOW REMAINS ANY PLACE, SHE SULKS ALL DAY AND REFUSES TO STEP *OUTSIDE* HER ROOM."

"TO KEEP HER HAPPY THE KING PASSED A LAW FINING ANYONE WHO FAILS TO KEEP HIS PROPERTY ABSOLUTELY *BARE* OF SNOW."

Proclamation

"BUT NO MATTER HOW HARD WE TRY... SWEEPING, SHOVELING AND BRUSHING, IT'S *IMPOSSIBLE* TO CLEAR AWAY EVERY *SINGLE* SNOWFLAKE."

AND SO NOW THE KING HAS DECIDED TO BUILD A GLASS DOME SO NO SNOW CAN FALL ON THE TOWN.

IT'S TERRIBLE BECAUSE WE HAVE ALWAYS *LOVED* SNOW.

GREAT SHINY SNOWFLAKES! I SHOULD THINK A LOT HAPPIER SOLUTION WOULD BE TO TEACH THE QUEEN TO *LIKE* SNOW.

A LOVELY NOTION MY DEAR SNOWMAN, BUT *QUITE* IMPOSSIBLE.

IF ONLY I COULD GET TO TALK TO HER!

YOU...A *SNOW-MAN!* YOU COULD NOT GET PASSED THE PALACE GATES.

360

362

365

370

Starry Night Publishing

Everyone has a story...

Don't spend your life trying to get published! Don't tolerate rejection! Don't do all the work and allow the publishing companies reap the rewards!

Millions of independent authors like you, are making money, publishing their stories now. Our technological know-how will take the headaches out of getting published. Let "Starry Night Publishing.Com" take care of the hard parts, so you can focus on writing. You simply send us your Word Document and we do the rest. It really is that simple!

The big companies want to publish only "celebrity authors," not the average book-writer. It's almost impossible for first-time authors to get published today. This has led many authors to go the self-publishing route. Until recently, this was considered "vanity-publishing." You spent large sums of your money, to get twenty copies of your book, to give to relatives at Christmas, just so you could see your name on the cover. Now, however, the self-publishing industry allows authors to get published in a timely fashion, retain the rights to your work, keeping up to ninety-percent of your royalties, instead of the traditional five-percent.

We've opened up the gates, allowing you inside the world of publishing. While others charge you as much as fifteen-thousand dollars for a publishing package, we charge less than five-hundred dollars to cover copyright, ISBN, and distribution costs. Do you really want to spend all your time formatting, converting, designing a cover, and then promoting your book, because no one else will?

Our editors are professionals, able to create a top-notch book that you will be proud of. Becoming a published author is supposed to be fun, not a hassle.

At Starry Night Publishing, you submit your work, we create a professional-looking cover, a table of contents, compile your text and images into the appropriate format, convert your files for eReaders, take care of copyright information, assign an ISBN, allow you to keep one-hundred-percent of your rights, distribute your story worldwide on Amazon, Barnes & Noble and many other retailers, and write you a check for your royalties. There are no other hidden fees involved! You don't pay extra for a cover, or to keep your book in print. We promise! Everything is included! You even get a free copy of your book and unlimited half-price copies.

In nine short years, we've published more than four thousand books, compared to the major publishing houses which only add an average of six new titles per year. We will publish your fiction, or non-fiction books about anything, and look forward to reading your stories and sharing them with the world.

We sincerely hope that you will join the growing Starry Night Publishing family, become a published author and gain the world-wide exposure that you deserve. You deserve to succeed. Success comes to those who make opportunities happen, not those who wait for opportunities to happen. You just have to try. Thanks for joining us on our journey.

www.starrynightpublishing.com

www.facebook.com/starrynightpublishing/

Made in the USA
Middletown, DE
13 November 2020